dark nebulae

by John J. Dunphy

illustrations by 7ARS

Dark Nebulae
by John J. Dunphy

First Printing, January 2009
Second Printing, March 2018
Third Printing, March 2024

Hiraeth Publishing
P.O. Box 1248
Tularosa, NM 88352

e-mail: hiraethsubs@yahoo.com

Visit www.hiraethsffh.com for online science fiction, fantasy, horror, scifaiku, and more. While you are there, visit the Shop for paperbacks, magazines, and chapbooks. **Support the small, independent press...**

For Charlie and Mr. Otts

Introduction

I try to avoid doing introductions. When I encounter them in other works, I usually turn the pages until I can get to the meat of the book, the actual work for which I bought the book in the first place. I have this aversion because I prefer to make up my own mind, and form my own opinions. By and large, I don't care what anyone else thinks about a particular work.

And yet . . . the merits of some works are not always as apparent as they are in others. Such is the case with the work of John Dunphy. He excels in a form of writing—of poetry, to be fair—with which most readers are unfamiliar, to wit: haibun. A haibun, briefly, is a short story or passage punctuated by one or more poems, usually haiku, sometimes tanka. Because we publish only science fiction, fantasy, and horror, these haiku necessarily take a science fiction or fantasy tack, and are therefore referred to as scifaiku.

To put it simply: John Dunphy = haibun.

In here you will find short tales of laughter and tears, of dawns and dusks, of Goth chicks and chick flicks, of heroes, villains, and lots of grays. You'll also find visions and ideas for you to contemplate and perhaps apply in some way to your life—which is, after all, one of the fundamental purposes of literature. As for making you a wee bit uncomfortable, well, that's another purpose.

Welcome to Dark Nebulae. Remember: there is a way out. Just close the book—if you can.

Tyree Campbell
Managing Editor
HiraethPublishing

dark nebulae

Late Hours

Unlike many of my spoiled brat classmates, I'm putting myself through college. Since I work late afternoons and evenings, I use the library from 11 until it closes at 3 in the morning.

The library is pretty empty at this hour. The students who don't have to work are in the dorms pounding their pillows. Still, there are usually a few other night owls in the library. Such as the girl I've named the Babe in Black. A real Goth chick who always wears a tight, black leather top and pants as well as shiny black boots. Long, straight black hair, white make-up, lips painted so red they look like little fire trucks — we're talking totally hot!

There she is now, sitting in a corner chair reading — oh, this is just too much — a thick, old leather-bound book!   Babe in Black really believes in staying in character!

So I have to work my way through college. Working-class guys have needs, too.   I don't get to meet many coeds with my job schedule. Tonight, I'm going to check out Babe in Black.

"Hi, fellow night owl!   How's it going?"   Hey, she's turning to look at me! She's getting up! She's smiling at me! Yeah!

You've got to be kidding. She's had her teeth filed into points! Wait until I tell the guys tomorrow at work!

    restaurant manager
    tells the police about
    his missing server

Space Dump

The dumping ground — that's what we call this planet. Periodically, the Ruling Elders decide that some plant or animal poses a threat to our ecosystem. Since destroying living entities is abhorrent to us, it's the Disposal Unit's job to transport the entities to the dumping ground.

Did I mention that the dumping ground planet is inhabited by indigenous animals and plants? Thanks to us, it's also teeming with alien life forms.

    South America
    scientists discover
    a new species of monkey

Main Course

She lives in a small, isolated cabin on the bayou. There are no other cabins nearby because the other Cajuns and Creoles are afraid of her.

Her cabin is crammed with bottles and jars holding objects that defy identification or even description. Candles burn before statues that once depicted the Virgin and other saints. The figures have been repainted and even physically altered into bizarre and terrifying images.

The old woman prayed before one of these statues for the better part of a day and a night. Muttering words in Cajun French, she's now removing with one gnarled hand a rooster from its cage. In her other hand, she grasps a knife with a blade that has been inscribed with incomprehensible symbols.

The chicken is swiftly decapitated.

> Baton Rouge formal dinner party —
> guests scream as their host
> loses his head

Final Fare

I drove a taxi for eighteen years. The money was good and it beat being cooped up in an office or factory. I thought I would stick with it until I retired.

But I quit last Autumn.

I picked up this guy in a seedy neighborhood and was driving him to an address in the loft district. He was so quiet in the back seat that I checked my rear-view mirror to see if he had fallen asleep. After dropping him off, I drove back to company headquarters and gave my notice.

    the man
    in my back seat
    casting no reflection

The Sin Eater

There was a sin eater in our Welsh village. He ate a crust of bread and drank from a cup of ale that had been passed over the corpse. The transgressions of the dead man or woman thereby passed into the sin eater.

Our village's sin eater has been dead over a half century, but the soil of his grave is still barren of grass and even weeds. The villagers say nothing can grow on his grave because all the sins carried in his corpse forever poisoned the soil. Even birds never alight on the grave, since folks say not even a worm can live in that ground.

As an experiment, I scattered some breadcrumbs on the sin eater's grave to see if I could lure some birds. After some time, a bird finally flew down to explore the crumbs. But a few seconds later —

> sin eater's grave —
> an alighted bird
> drops dead

The Aristocrat of the Graveyard

Baron Cimetiere (pronounced "cemetery") is a powerful Voodoo loa of the dead. He and his wife, Brigitte, are the guardian spirits of that crossroads where souls pass from life to....well, we would say death, but adherents of Voodoo would say to another life. As a nobleman, one can expect a degree of gentility from Baron Cimetiere not commonly found in the spirit world.

spirit world —
Baron Cimetiere bows to kiss
a new arrival's hand

Alien Invasion

The glowing mother ship hovered just a few yards above his head. Scores of tiny vessels darted around it at hyperspeed.

He knew the Earth couldn't possibly withstand this extraterrestrial assault, but he was determined to go down fighting.

2am
drunk hurls a rock
at the streetlight

The Teacher

He was a good man, especially by Earthling standards. They are a violent species and seem to take enjoyment in tormenting and killing each other. But he was different. He tried to teach them to forsake violence and concern themselves with one another's well being.

I say "tried to teach them" because, as one might expect, they killed him. I was able to reanimate his body, which returned him to life as his species knows it. His teachings were important and remarkably advanced for a human. Members of his species could only benefit from hearing a bit more of what he had to say.

But I know these beings. After all, I've studied them for hundreds of their years. And they would only have slain him again. It's simply their nature.

So I beamed him aboard my spacecraft shortly after reanimating him. Of course, Earthlings have no knowledge of such matters and interpreted the teacher's vanishing as magic.

    followers watch
    Jesus ascend
    into heaven

Master of the Runes

I experimented with runes for years before achieving success. By arranging rune-inscribed cubes in this pattern, I can open the gates of hell and summon a demon to do my bidding. Have you seen that 1950s-era horror film that portrayed a sorcerer who could perform such a feat? Well, that was fiction. This is fact.

There is one important similarity between myself and that movie character, however. We both use the demon to dispose of our enemies in a delightfully grisly manner.

My demon should be returning any moment now, having torn to pieces my rival for a young woman's affection. This runic pattern not only summons the demon to do my bidding but also ensures that it cannot harm me. If the pattern were altered even slightly, I would be as vulnerable to the creature's claws and fangs as any of my victims.

I hear footsteps outside. It has returned, and now it's back to hell for the demon until I need it again.

What was that? What's happening? My runes! The pattern!

      all lightweight objects
      moved
      by the earthquake

The Family Man

When our son told us he had fallen in love with an alien and intended to marry her, my wife and I were apprehensive. Oh, we're not prejudiced, but many other humans still are, and we knew that our son and his beloved would have a rough time of it.

My wife and I count the day that we were presented with our first grandchild as one of the happiest of our long life together. When I held that precious baby in my arms at the hospital, I wept tears of joy — and I pride myself in being a tough guy! Well, I am a tough guy, and any bigot who tries to give grief to this darling little girl will have an irate grandpa to contend with. So she's half-alien. She's also half-human on our son's side!

> half-alien grandchild —
> our son's eyes
> his wife's antennae

Down Yonder

Great-grandma told us about a strange experience her pa had in the Ozark hill country. He was coon hunting one full-moon night when his sturdy hunting dog suddenly hid behind him and started whining like a baby. Then great-great-grandpa saw it: a big wolf with glowing red eyes. At first, he thought it was holding a rag doll in its mouth. But rag dolls don't drip blood.

Enraged by such a vicious killing, he aimed his ten-gauge at the wolf and let it have both barrels. The wolf took off, still holding its prey, and disappeared into the woods.

A couple of days later, great-great grandpa was walking to the settlement when he passed an old woman who had a reputation for being able to do what the hill folks called "strange things." A chill passed through his body.

the witch woman —
her face and arms wrapped
in bloody bandages

The Dealer

Nicknamed Digger, he was a notorious dealer in Native American relics who had made good money plundering burial mounds in search of artifacts that he sold to collectors around the globe. Everyone who had worked with Digger during an excavation remarked about his cavalier attitude toward the Indian dead. Bones and skulls were scattered everywhere.

Digger's housekeeper found him dead in his study, just two days before he was scheduled to fly to the south-eastern United States to excavate another burial mound. His body was covered in blood. But it was his face that so intrigued the CSI team. Digger's mouth was agape in a silent scream, while his eyes looked as though they had glimpsed the very devil himself. What had he seen that had so terrified him?

The coroner's report was ordered sealed by the state police, but the story eventually leaked out.

imbedded in
the grave robber's body
stone arrowheads

Wrong Place, Wrong Time

"Deep night, dark night, the silent of the night,
The time of night when Troy was set on fire,
The time when screech owls cry and bandogs howl,
And spirits walk, and ghosts break up their graves —
That time best fits the work we have in hand."
                    - Shakespeare, Henry IV, Part 2

I owe my job to some stupid kids. The city fathers got sick and tired of the idiocy that was going on in this cemetery at night. Tombstones toppled over for use as altars in rituals, symbols and circles spray-painted on the ground, even some old graves dug up and bones scattered around.   I get $100 a night to walk around with a flashlight to make sure this craziness stops.

And speaking of craziness, just what's going on over there?   It's the kids — the first time I've actually caught them in the act!   I'll call the police on my cell phone, but first I'm going to sneak up and scare the hell out of them!

"All right, break it up!   Fun's over!   Now it's time to get your asses kicked, you little freaks!"

Hey, they aren't kids!   No matter — I'm still going to kick their asses before I call the cops.

"Okay, smart guy, what do you mean, 'Now we've got what we need.' ?"

    dawn
    sprawled across a tombstone
    man without a heart

Elusive Destination

I don't understand it. True, it's been some time since I visited the planet its inhabitants call Earth, but a landmass that size simply does not vanish! I'll check my coordinates again and traverse the quadrant one final time.

> alien spacecraft
> its commander searches
> for Atlantis

The Corpse Candle

It was said in old Wales that a corpse candle was always a harbinger of death. The corpse candle resembled a flame without a torch and the path it traced marked a journey of death. To see this eerie light move from a home to the cemetery meant that someone in the house would soon die and be buried in that very graveyard. To be followed by a corpse candle was an even more terrifying experience, since it meant that you were marked for death.

The only thing worse than seeing a corpse candle was seeing two.

> corpse candles
> moving from the house
> with twins

Transformation

I had heard that you're never the same after your first space flight. Now I know it's true.

There were 15 of us on the craft. We represented 15 nations and six continents. As we stood before the observation window and watched the Earth recede, some of us were able to identify our respective nations. A few seconds later, we could identify only our continents. Finally, there was just our beautiful planet, from which we were departing with such speed.

When the Earth ultimately disappeared from sight, I looked at my fellow voyagers and felt an intense kinship with them such as I had previously known only with members of my immediate family. I formerly had thought of my nationality as American and my race as white. I now thought of my nationality as Earthling and my race as human. Each of my shipmates experienced a similar epiphany.

> meal time in space
> at the center of our table
> a globe of Earth

A Little Love

My grandmother told me about them when I was a child. "The Pixies are little folks," she said. "Wee people who like to play tricks on us."

"Grandma, that's just a silly Old Country superstition," I proudly replied. "There's no such thing as a Pixie."

"It's the ones like you who don't believe in them that the Pixies usually trick," Grandma admonished me. "You'd better watch your step, young man!"

Well, I never watched my step as a child or adult....until last May Day morning.

I took a magnifying glass to check my bonsai trees to see if they were developing any new branches. And that's when I saw it. Now I not only believe in Pixies but know they have emotions very much like ours.

      carved on my bonsai —
      two sets of initials
      within an arrow-pierced heart

Just Passing Through

Our quantum physics professor had talked about parallel universes that evening, and Lucinda and I were discussing the subject as we walked to our dorm.   "Let me get this straight," she said.   "There are multiple universes that co-exist completely independent of each other?" she asked.

"That's the way I understand it," I replied. "In other words, a train from another universe could be running through us right now.   Or maybe we're at the bottom of the ocean of still another universe."

Lucinda laughed and held her nose, as though she were under water.   "How about a nice ocean bass for dinner?" I asked while pretending to snatch a fish out of the air.

"Hey, watch it!" Lucinda yelled as I suddenly grabbed her to keep from falling.   I had stumbled over something. But what? There was nothing on the sidewalk.

"Come on, Mr. Sure-Foot," she said.   "Let's get back to the dorm before you break a leg."

We laughed at my clumsiness.

    beach
    a solitary sunbather feels
    a kick to her side

Never Assume

My wife and I were hiking through the North Woods when we came upon an old stone bridge that spanned a swift stream. "Look at that!" my wife laughed as she pointed at the crudely painted sign. "The hicks up here can't even spell!"

"And if it's a toll bridge, where's the attendant to take our fare?" I added. "I guess things are just more laid-back in the sticks!"

We started across the bridge, still laughing. About midway, we froze. Oh, they know how to spell, I thought through my rising panic.

> walking toward us
> across the bridge
> a troll

On The Job

Don't get me wrong — I have nothing against aliens. I've worked with many of them on construction sites, and they've never given me any grief.

I can understand why management hires them. With the number of arms they've got, aliens were made for construction jobs. And what huge arms they are. Sure, they're great workers. It's just that it takes them so long to get started!

> noon
> the alien laborers
> still rolling up their sleeves

Bundle Of Joy

My husband and I enjoyed taking part in the monthly full moon hikes that were sponsored by our local Sierra Club. The path we took wound through a wooded area owned by a local naturalist.

There were about a dozen of us on the October hike. We had paused to gaze into the night sky, trying to identify the fall constellations, when we were attacked.

The creature moved so swiftly that none of us could get a clear look at it. But I felt fur when it knocked me down. I also felt its teeth sink into my arm. One of the hikers struck its head with a heavy flashlight, and the creature released me from its grip and bolted off. I later learned that my husband had been badly bitten as well.

If my husband and I want to know what the creature that attacked us looked like, all we now have to do is stare into one of our house mirrors when our transformation occurs during the full moon. But this isn't the worst of it, as we recently discovered.

> delivery room
> hospital staff recoils from
> our fur-covered newborn

The Observer

I enjoy studying the Earth beings that call themselves human. Technologically and intellectually, they're quite primitive compared to the inhabitants of other planets in Sector 4, but we can learn so much about our past by scrutinizing them. Disturbing as it is to admit, we ourselves were once at the stage of development now occupied by humans.

For the longest time, though, I dared not move among them. Humans call non-inhabitants of their planet "aliens" and "extraterrestrials" and fear them. The challenge for me was to interact freely with humans without causing the kind of panic that would skew my research.

Then, I discovered an Earth milieu that allows me to circulate undetected. My only concern is that the humans I encounter might not be representative of their planet's inhabitants as a whole,

> an alien
> chatting with costumed participants
> at the science fiction convention

Help From Above

I was piloting my spacecraft one night on a reconnaissance mission over the planet its inhabitants call Earth when I spotted a large fire. I know that we have been forbidden to interfere in their affairs without specific authorization, but these Earthlings are so primitive. Don't I have the moral obligation to save their lives and resources, if I'm in a position to do so?

So yes, I misted the blaze, and I refuse to apologize for it. Earthlings need all the help our people can give them.

> Ku Klux Klan rally —
> Klansmen try to re-ignite
> their extinguished cross

No Place Like Home

An ancestor, whose name I bear, co-founded a Habitat for Humanity affiliate in 1990 and served as secretary of its board of directors for the first eight years of its existence. Since then, at least one member of my family has always been involved with that very worthwhile organization.

That earlier John J. Dunphy would be so proud to know that Habitat still exists and continues to build houses for the underprivileged. But could he possibly imagine to what degree Habitat has extended its wonderful work since his day?

> ribbon-cutting ceremony
> Habitat dedicates its first house
> on another planet

As Then, So Now . . . And Forever

She had always wanted to be a vampire: to gain incredible power, to slay at will and — most of all — to live forever. So, unlike others who had been the unwilling prey of the denizens of the night, she had deliberately sought out one of the undead and offered him her neck.

Now, she too sucked blood and eschewed the sun. And she would never die.

But she hadn't realized that, once made into a vampire, the new predator was frozen in time, bound to remain in her or his form when the transformation from mortal to immortal had occurred. A child made into a vampire would always be a child. An elderly person made into a vampire would forever be gray-haired and wrinkled. And her damned soul would forever inhabit the body that had been hers when she had joined the ranks of the undead.

daybreak
beside the vampire's coffin
her empty wheelchair

The Star Gazer

"Tis now the very witching time of night,
When churchyards yawn and hell itself breathes out
Contagion to the world."

-Shakespeare, Hamlet

Let's get one thing straight right off the bat: I'm not some kind of weirdo who enjoys hanging out in cemeteries. It's just that I live in a city where the only unobstructed view of the night sky that an astronomy buff can get is in the local cemetery. Besides, the cemetery caretaker is a buddy and I always let him know when I'll be out there.

Word on the Net was that a new comet would be visible from where I live, but on one night only. I asked Jeff, the cemetery caretaker, if I could set up my telescope on that night and he said no problem. In fact, he said he might join me, since he had always wanted to see a comet. Jeff laughed and added he had heard astronomy could really build up a thirst, so he'd show up with a six-pack.

About midnight, I felt a tap on my shoulder. With my eye still glued to the telescope, I asked Jeff to pass me a beer. When no beer was forthcoming, I turned around to get it myself.

pointing at me
a finger
with no flesh

Color Him Swell

My promotion with its accompanying salary hike allowed me to purchase that spacecraft I'd had my eye on for months. Lightweight but sturdy, with every conceivable accessory — oh man, I knew I'd be the envy of the neighborhood. But I honestly never guessed to what degree.

When I tried to show off my new baby, the neighbors got downright vicious! One of my oldest friends sneered and said that I must think I'm too good to fly the junk heaps everybody else around here is content with! Virtually no one shared my joy upon acquiring my dream spacecraft.

I say "virtually no one" because there was a notable — and surprising — exception. The only alien in the neighborhood shook my hand with his...well, "hand" for lack of a better word, and warmly congratulated me. He didn't express a trace of resentment and was genuinely happy for me. All right, so maybe this alien guy looks a little weird by narrow-minded Earth standards, but he's okay in my book.

> my alien neighbor
> green
> but not with envy

Fresh Game

"Lord, we know who we are, but know not what we may be."

- Shakespeare, Hamlet

I was a jack-lighter, just like my daddy before him and his daddy before him. For the benefit of you city folks, a jack-lighter hunts deer at night by shining a big flashlight beam on them. The deer freeze, just like they do when your car's headlights strike them, and then you shoot. It's illegal, of course, but backwoods folks have been doing it for years. It keeps meat on the family table, and you make a little money selling the extra venison to stores that don't ask too many questions.

My boy had fixed the flashlight beam on a young doe when something attacked him. The flashlight busted when he dropped it, and I couldn't see much in the dark. But I sure heard poor Tom screaming as whatever it was tore him apart. Then it tackled me.

The thing knocked me down and my rifle went flying. I managed to draw my hunting knife and rammed it into the beast's side. It screamed, jumped off me and ran into the woods. I had teeth and claw marks galore but managed to crawl home.

My wounds healed, and I'm able to hunt again. But I don't go after deer anymore.

    full moon
    I creep toward the tourist cabin
    on all fours

Across The Abyss

I never thought I'd attend a séance, but now I'm grasping at straws. Since we were parted, all I've wanted to do is communicate with my wife to let her know how much I miss her and still love her — and always will.

So here I am, joining hands with other grieving men, women and even children, all of whom are desperate to break through to the other side. I doubt whether this will work, but I've at least got to try. Oh, darling, I've miss you so much since I died!

> awakened at 2 am —
> widow thinks she hears
> her husband's voice

First Warning

I was taking my evening walk when I saw an eerie green light throbbing from the other side of the hill. I went over to investigate and then froze in terror. It was one of those UFOs that I've heard people talk about.

A doorway of the spaceship opened, and these things got out. I call them "things" because they certainly weren't like any humans or animals that I've ever seen. I don't know what they want here, but I'm willing to bet it's nothing good for us!

And now I'm running as fast as these old legs can take me. I've got to warn my family, but how will I ever make them understand what I've seen?

> living room —
> kids tell their panting dog
> to stop barking

The Confessor

Some call me the Vicar of Hell, while others know me as Chaplain to the Damned. I prefer the simple appellation "the Confessor."

My Lord Lucifer has authorized me to roam the world, listen to the confessions of those pledged to serve him and grant them absolution for their transgressions. I must congratulate myself on devising some astonishingly original penances for those who sin against my Lord.

This demon decidedly enjoys his work.

You might think that it's impossible for Luciferian mortals to sin, but I quite assure you that's not the case. There is a well-defined code of morality that they are expected to follow to the letter.

When they violate that code, they must seek absolution from the Confessor or accept the consequences. Since no one in their right mind wants to accept these kind of consequences, Luciferian mortals humbly seek the absolution that only I can offer.

> Black Rite of Absolution —
> a Luciferian mortal confesses
> his good deeds

Death On The Range

Since becoming a werewolf six years ago, I have killed with impunity during the full moon. Ranchers, cowboys, outlaws, Indians — it made no difference to me. A few quick-draw gunfighters managed to get off a shot or two, merely to discover that lead bullets have no effect on my kind. An old Mexican woman with knowledge of the dark arts told me that only a silver bullet can slay a werewolf.

I spied a white man and an Indian riding through the canyon. I sprang on the Indian, knocked him from his horse and was just about to rip open his throat when I felt a burning pain in my chest.

The white man had shot me. Blood oozed from the deadly wound, and I fell to the ground.

My strength is ebbing away, but I can see the white man helping the Indian to his feet.

I don't understand it! Lead bullets can't harm me! What kind of Westerner would load his revolver with silver bullets?

> dying —
> I manage to snarl at
> the masked man

Double Standard

The Earthlings who speak the language known as English call it graffiti. It refers to any kind of unauthorized writing or artwork in a public place. When Earthlings discover graffiti that other Earthlings have created, they simply obliterate it and that's the end of the matter. Why, then, do they become so distraught when we imitate them by creating some graffiti?

farmer's field —
police and scientists investigate
crop circles

Tourist Trap

My idiotic tour guide said that no trip to New Orleans is complete without witnessing an authentic Voodoo ceremony, and I fell for it. I can't believe I'm actually standing around watching a bunch of wackos in an old cemetery at midnight when I could be partying in the French Quarter!

"Hey, witch doctors or whatever the hell you call yourselves, let's hurry it up! 1 want to get out of here and check out the babes at the strip clubs!"

Man, that one old hag is giving me a dirty look......

Crescent City voodoo shop —
hanging in the window
a doll without a mouth

Smallpox Island

A prison in my Mississippi River hometown of Alton, Illinois housed Confederate POWs during the Civil War. When smallpox broke out, ailing inmates were transferred to an isolation hospital on a small island near the prison. Prisoners who died at the hospital were buried on the island. After the war, townspeople began calling the site Smallpox Island.

Some Altonians claimed the island was haunted. Many years ago, according to one account, some local boys decided to demonstrate their fearlessness by spending the night on Smallpox Island. They built a campfire and soon drifted off to sleep.

The boys were awakened about midnight by footsteps. The embers of their dying campfire provided just enough light to see who was approaching.

in tattered uniforms
gaunt men
with pox-scarred faces

Swept Away

When news of the impending hurricane reached us, the entire community — including my family — evacuated the area. I, however, chose to stay. I've always been daring, and the opportunity to witness the power of nature in all its raw fury was just too much to resist.

And now, I rue that foolish decision with all my heart and soul. The hurricane swept me away.

I know I can't survive much longer. I only hope that my battered, torn body will be returned home when I die.

> New Orleans
> rescue workers peer at
> the beached mermaid

And Baby Makes Three

My husband, Tom, and I mutually detest what passes for modern civilization and decided to move to the woods. Our water source is a well, while candles and lanterns light our cabin, which we built without power tools. We grow and hunt all our food. Meals are cooked on a wood-burning stove.

When I became pregnant, Tom delivered the baby himself. Our dark-eyed, dark-haired darling grew fat on breast-milk, and we thought life couldn't possibly get any better. Then, seven months after her birth, our baby died.

I thought I was going to die, too. I couldn't eat, couldn't sleep, couldn't work. For days at a time, I would sit in my rocking chair by the fireplace and cry.

One day, when Tom came home from hunting, he placed a baby into my grieving arms. Tom told me that he had found the child abandoned in a cabin miles away. This poor little girl needed parents, he said, and it was up to us to raise her as our own.

No more days and nights of mourning for this mother. I'm too busy caring for my baby! I love her as though she were my own flesh and blood. She even has dark eyes and hair like the baby I lost.

> fireside
> woman rocks and sings to
> a baby Sasquatch

Student Life

I was reading an ancestor's memoir the other day and was struck by her account of university studies in the twentieth century. It goes without saying that her literature classes were devoted only to the works of Earth authors. I wonder what she would think about one of her descendants majoring in literature by non-human authors. She wrote that her history classes were challenging because "there's just so much to remember." Students today are required to learn all the facts and dates that were contained in those old hardcopy textbooks she used -- plus all the facts and dates of the three centuries since my ancestor was a student!

She wrote about really enjoying her World Religions class and how it expanded her appreciation for other cultures. I just wish my ancestor could sit in on a class I'm taking this semester. Her appreciation for other cultures would really be expanded.

> University of Mars
> student completes a term paper
> for Galactic Religions class

Head Over Heels

With its history of running those women-of-this and women-of-that pictorials, I knew it was just a matter of time before Playboy came up with the idea of a "Women of Outer Space" layout. I heard that something like 400 women auditioned for selection as models. I'm so excited to have been chosen!

As the photographer was saying, the basics of a Playboy shoot don't change — beautiful young woman, nude or nearly so and immaculate attention to hair and make-up. At zero-gravity, though, the poses are what's going to blow everyone's minds.

spacecraft photo shoot —
model begins another
slow motion somersault

Reunion

I never knew my parents and grew up in a series of foster homes, each one worse than the one before.   If I had brothers and sisters, I don't remember them. I joined the army when I turned 18 and was sent to Vietnam.   A million-dollar wound got me a ticket back to the States, but not before I saw things and did things that haunt me to this day.   Booze and drugs landed me in county jails and state prisons in three states before they finally diagnosed me as having post-traumatic stress syndrome.

The meds they put me on helped some, but I could never hold a job for very long.   I tried marriage three times with no luck. At 59, I'm back in the hospital. This time, though, it's not for getting drunk and picking a fight with a stranger.   I'm dying of cancer.

I've heard that, when you die, a loved one returns to greet you and accompanies you to the other side.   Well, who the hell would come for me?   No one ever gave a damn about me, and I never gave much of a damn for anyone.

Oh, what difference does it make?   There's probably no life after death anyway.

I'm so tired.....

I must have drifted off to sleep for a moment. Hey, what the hell?

    curled up beside me —
    that stray dog I fed
    thirty years ago

The Union Organizer

The labor movement in the United States has remained powerful and relevant by changing with the times. Craft unions predominated in the nineteenth century. The American Federation of Labor brought these unions together into one powerful organization that earned the respect of business and government.

Heavy industrialization in the early twentieth century created a large mass of workers in the manufacturing sector, such as automobile, rubber and steel. The Industrial Workers of the World and, later, the Congress of Industrial Organizations organized these workers into powerful - and sometimes radical - industrial unions.

Most American manufacturing jobs were shipped overseas in the late twentieth and early twenty-first centuries. So the labor movement shifted gears and began organizing fast-food employees and retail workers. It was a struggle to organize the Wal-Mart chain, but we eventually succeeded.

Now, in the twenty-second century, the labor movement has again changed the focus of its organizing drives. We're now reaching out to that segment of the population engaged in the most dangerous and demeaning occupations in the United States. We're focusing on sanitation workers, domestic employees, nuclear energy workers and, yes, even sex industry workers. The contemporary labor movement is determined to organize those at the very bottom of the socio-economic pyramid. We want to win a better life for the unappreciated, shamefully-exploited workers who toil in the very worst jobs.

I know what their lives are like because I come from their ranks. That's precisely why the American Labor

Congress hired me.   Who better to help organize these workers than one of them?

    labor rally
    the organizer harangues
    his fellow androids

Crash Landing

My spacecraft's life-support system as well as its propulsion unit failed. I crash-landed on a planet that I was only vaguely familiar with.

I knew I was dying when I pulled myself from the wreckage. Although I had never particularly feared death, the thought of ending my existence on an alien planet so far away from my home and loved ones horrified me.

Stumbling from my craft, I surveyed the terrain with eyes already beginning to glaze over.   I couldn't believe what I saw!   For just a moment, I thought God had heard my prayer and miraculously transported me home.

It was the landscape of my planet, and it was here in this strange world across the galaxy!   Such beauty would make anyone's death bearable.

With what little strength I have left, I'm going to crawl about and think of home. When death comes, it will find me with a glad spirit and a joyful heart.

    on all fours
    an alien drags himself
    across Antarctica

Fish for Dinner

The best fishing hole is just downstream from where Pastor Jimmy baptizes the new members of his congregation. Some of them old boys must have raised some powerful hell before joining the church because, after a baptism, their washed-away sins drift downstream and end up in the fishing hole. Whenever I see a fish or two floating in the water, I know they were poisoned by those washed-away sins.

You think I'm funning you? Well, I'll let you in a little secret. I was married to the meanest woman in the world for darned near thirty years. One day I decided I couldn't take no more. Pastor Jimmy baptized one of the worst moon shiners in the hills and, before too long, a big old catfish was floating dead.   I took that sin-soaked fish home for dinner, but you can bet I didn't eat a bite of it.

> dinner table
> the dead woman face-down
> on a half-eaten catfish

Politics as Usual

When aliens began immigrating to Earth, I fully supported their right to settle here. I also supported their right to become naturalized citizens of the respective countries that they chose to call home. And yes, when they expressed the desire to seek elective offices, I lined up behind that as well. Why not? If they paid taxes and registered to vote, it seemed only fair that they be allowed to participate in the electoral process.

But I didn't foresee the tremendous advantage that their anatomy would give them in a political campaign. All the human candidates are crying foul, since they're unable to keep pace with the alien candidates. The simple truth is that, with bodies like theirs, aliens were born to run for public office.

> the alien candidate
> shaking hands with voters
> six at a time

Working Abroad

The Earth Employment Agency on my planet promised us steady work if we immigrated to Earth. I can still hear the manager who recruited us saying that, with our unique physiques, we would never be out of work on his planet.

Perhaps I should explain that, by "unique physiques," he was referring to our torsos. We're shaped a great deal like the geometric figure that Earthlings call a rectangle.

Well, the manager didn't lie to us. We have steady work, all right. But it's a job that most Earthlings consider demeaning and just plain boring.

> sidewalk
> the pacing alien's torso painted
> EAT AT JOE'S

All in a Day's Work

I'm a witch who specializes in making the lives of my targeted women and men an absolute hell on Earth. What have these people done to me? Nothing whatsoever! My clients pay me to persecute them — and they pay me well indeed. Since I'm very good at what I do, they always get their money's worth.

Want to get even with someone who has wronged you? Pay me ten grand and then send the offending party my way. I'll do the rest. True, I need some personal item of theirs to make the mayhem possible, but acquiring it presents no challenge for me. This smart witch has the perfect cover job.

    witch
    clips her new target's hair
    in the salon

Hell Freezing Over

He ruined my daughter. I know you city folks laugh about such matters, but we don't joke about things like that here in the hill country. When some city boy uses my daughter for his own pleasure and then casts her aside when he's done with her, this hill daddy don't laugh. He gets even.

And getting even is easy when you're a witch-man like me.

I made me a poppit. If you ever see one, you lowlanders would say a poppit looks like those home-made dolls they sell at craft fairs. Well, dolls are for little girls' fun, and there ain't nothing fun about a poppit. A poppit is for hurting someone and hurting them real bad.

I said the spell-words over the poppit so that smooth city slicker would feel just what it felt. When the old-timers did something like this, they used the icehouse. Well, we're citified now and got electricity just like you lowlanders. So I put the poppit in the freezer.

> city street
> a young man dies of hypothermia
> in August

On The Road

I've traveled to the far regions of galaxies and seen phenomena that a primitive species such as Earthlings can neither comprehend nor even imagine. Today, however, I'm on their planet — incognito, of course. The journey I intend to take is ridiculously short. It will encompass just slightly over 2,000 units of the measurement that Earthlings on this segment of land mass commonly call a mile.

Still, I could hardly be more excited! Since my species began monitoring Earth broadcasts, I've been intrigued by this path that has been described by so many Earthlings who have traveled it. Today, I will travel it, and I will do so in a vehicle designed by the Earthlings themselves for the specific purpose of terrestrial exploration.

> leased '65 Mustang —
> an alien drives
> Route 66

Blue And Gray

I'm glad that so many Americans are eager to learn more about the Civil War. These reenactments of famous battles always draw large crowds.

I try to witness as many Civil War reenactments as I can, and I'm generally impressed. The re-enactors appear to pay great attention to the most minute details in the interest of accuracy. Their uniforms are much like the ones worn during the Civil War, while the battles are staged as they occurred so long ago.

Of course, the re-enactors who are "slain" simply get up from the battlefield and walk away when the event is concluded. That was an option my men and I were not afforded.

    Gettysburg
    tourist points to the officer
    wearing a bloody uniform

Facing One's Fear

I'm a man who simply cannot abide weaknesses in people, and I regard superstition as one of the very worst weaknesses that afflict humanity. When my new girlfriend told me about a superstition that cripples her, I told her there was but one thing to do — face it! That's the best way to overcome a fear!

And that's precisely what we're doing. Imagine the absurdity of being frightened of the full moon to the point of locking yourself in a room during those few nights! My girlfriend and I are taking a walk in the moonlight at this very moment.

walking hand-in-hand —
his girlfriend's skin
suddenly feeling furry

The Rebel

Do you know what it's like not to own your body? You say you have no idea?   Then you're obviously not a clone.

The cloning of human beings became legal when wealthy people realized that it would afford them an opportunity to undo the damage they had done to their bodies through hedonism.   Destroy your liver and kidneys by alcoholism?   Get off to a fresh start by having your clone's organs implanted in your body.   Ruin your skin through sunbathing on the beaches of your private islands?   Kill your clone by having his or her skin removed and wear it as your own.   Heart and lungs no longer functional from decades of smoking?   Get replacements from your clone.   Fry your brain by experimenting with drugs?   Have your skull filled with your clone's brain.   Your new mind, nourished by those healthy brain cells, can be easily reformatted by any one of a number of computer programs currently on the market.

We clones are created for the sole purpose of providing spare parts for your bodies.   Our deaths — and we indeed die, although you choose not to employ that word when referring to us — mean another chance for you.   We perish unmourned, while you celebrate a new opportunity to take life by the horns.

I have chosen to rebel against my fate.

My "master," as I am required to call him, has been pickling his body for years with heavy drinking.   He already covets my kidneys and liver; in fact, he's told me that I shouldn't get too attached to them.   That's his idea of a joke.

Well, the joke will be on him when he has me killed and dissected for my organs. "Master" will soon join me in death because my kidneys and liver will be no good to him or any other human. I'm seeing to that!

night
the clone drinks
his master's liquor

About the author . . .

John J. Dunphy is the author of the scifaiku collection Stellar Possibilities (Alban Lake Publishing, 2006) as well as the haiku collection Old Soldiers Fading Away (Pudding House, 2006).   His scifaiku and haiku have appeared in Scifaikuest, the shantytown anomaly, Modern Haiku, Frogpond, bottle rockets and many other poetry journals.   His free verse has been published in The Mid-America Poetry Review and Springhouse.   Dunphy is the owner of The Second Reading Book Shop in Alton, Illinois. Visit him in cyberspace at www.johndunphy.com and
www.secondreadingbookshop.com

What???
No subscription to
Scifaikuest??

You'll miss more John
Dunphy!!! Oh, no!!!

But wait!
We can fix that . . .

https://www.hiraethsffh.com/product-
page/scifaikuest-1

And a subscription makes a
great gift, for a holiday or
any time of the year!

A Little Help, Please

In the world of the small indie press we fight a never-ending battle for attention to our work, as writers and in publishing. Here's an example: big publishers [you know who they are] have gobs of $$$ that they can devote to advertising and marketing. Here at Hiraeth Publishing, our advertising budget consists of the deposits for whatever soda bottles and aluminum cans we can find alongside the highways. Anti-littering laws make our task even more difficult . . . ☺

That's where YOU come in. YOU are our best promoter. YOU are the one who can tell others about us. Just send 'em to our website, tell them about our store. That's all. Just that.

Of course, we don't mind if you talk us up. We're pretty good, you know. We have some award-winning and award-nominated writers and artists, plus other voices well-deserving to be heard [not everyone wins awards, right?] but our publications are read-worthy nevertheless.

That number once again is:

www.hiraethsffh.com

Friend us on Facebook at Hiraeth Publish

Follow us on Twitter at

@hiraethpublish1

Stellar Possibilities
By John J. Dunphy

The master of combining flash stories with haiku is back, and this time he has a collection loaded with foibles, anecdotes, scifaiku, dreams, fantasies, and huh? what? If you've read an issue of Scifaikuest, you know his work. And if you don't know his work—you should get acquainted. Here are a couple pieces:

> archaeological exploration
> painted on a cave wall
> mushroom clouds

and

> quantum vacation
> the numbers on our hotel room
> keep changing

There are lots more inside . . .

https://www.hiraethsffh.com/product-page/stellar-possibilities-by-john-dunphy

Sentimental

A reclusive French anthropologist named Pierrette is visited by an extraterrestrial anthropologist named Canelle who wants to know about the relationship humans have with their "things"—flowers, collectibles, souvenirs, etc. Both women soon learn that there is more to relationships than meets the eye at first glance. But can a relationship between dedicated anthropologists from different worlds endure?

a $1.59 short story!
Winner of the specficworld writing contest!

ePub: https://www.hiraethsffh.com/product-page/sentimental-by-tyree-campbell